# Ready, Set –
# Regina!

*Other Avon Camelot Books by*
**Lynn Cullen**

THE BACKYARD GHOST
MEETING THE MAKE-OUT KING

LYNN CULLEN grew up in Fort Wayne, Indiana. She received a bachelor's degree from Indiana University and did postgraduate work in education at Mercer University and Georgia State University. Her other books include *The Backyard Ghost* and *Meeting the Make-out King*. She lives in Atlanta, Georgia, with her husband and three daughters.

# Ready, Set — Regina!

## LYNN CULLEN

AN AVON CAMELOT BOOK

READY, SET—REGINA! is an original publication of Avon Books. This work has never before appeared in book form.


AVON BOOKS
A division of
The Hearst Corporation
1350 Avenue of the Americas
New York, New York 10019

Copyright © 1996 by Lynn Cullen
Published by arrangement with the author
Library of Congress Catalog Card Number: 95-95105
ISBN: 0-380-78427-0
RL: 4.9

First Avon Camelot Printing: May 1996

CAMELOT TRADEMARK REG. U.S. PAT. OFF. AND IN OTHER COUNTRIES, MARCA REGISTRADA, HECHO EN U.S.A.

Printed in the U.S.A.

OPM   10  9  8  7  6  5  4  3  2  1

For Alison

Pride goeth before destruction
and a haughty spirit before a fall.

—Proverbs 16:18


You can't keep a funny girl down.

—Regina Calhoun

# 1

# The Bubble Gets Popped

The bubble collapsed with a fleshy *blam*. A sticky sheet of goo drifted over the face of Regina Calhoun.

"Re-GEE-na!" Mr. Amsden's voice boomed above the uproar of the cafeteria crowd at The Queen of Angels school.

Regina tried to blink in innocence, but the gum in her lashes made it difficult. The bubble had been well on its way to a spot in the *Guinness Book of World Records*. "Yes, sir?"

"That's one detention!"

Regina took the gum that remained in her mouth and used it to blot the mess off her eyes, giving her a clearer view of Mr. Amsden. He stood behind her best friend, Margaret, hands on hips. Though he was a balding, stout, short man—Regina's own mother towered above him at class parties—he seemed to have grown in the last few minutes.

"Why do you do it?" he asked. "Why do you do things that make me give you detentions?"

Regina glanced at Arley and Matthew, the boys sitting next to Margaret. They bent over their hands snickering. Wasn't it obvious? Why did she do anything? Humor, baby!

"I'll see you after school Monday," said Mr. Amsden.

"I've already got a detention then."

"All right, the next day."

"I've got one then, too."

Mr. Amsden's thick lips curved up, but it wasn't exactly a smile. "When *don't* you have a detention, Regina?"

"Tomorrow. Otherwise, I'm booked."

"Wonderful. Then tomorrow it is. Congratulations, Regina." Mr. Amsden stalked back to the teacher's table.

"Thank you," Regina said.

Arley and Matthew burst into guffaws. Regina glowed.

Behind her glasses, Margaret's gray eyes were round with concern. "Regina, what about the tryouts for the talent show?"

Regina ran her tongue over her chipped tooth. She had gotten the chipped tooth while racing Arley, Matthew, and Margaret on the blacktop last fall. While Matthew and Margaret were no threat—no way could Matthew move his adult size ten-and-a-halfs fast enough, and Margaret lacked guts—Arley claimed to be the fastest kid in the fifth grade. Regina had been a good two feet ahead of him when she tripped and fell.

Though her mother took her to the dentist, Regina

refused to have the tooth capped. Leaving the tooth jagged was like wearing an Olympic medal—a testimony to her moment of greatness.

"I heard Mr. Amsden give you a detention, Regina," said Kate, walking up with her lunch tray. "Guess you won't be able to try out for the talent show."

"Yeah, you won't get to sing," said Arley, tossing back his blanket of straight blonde hair to warble the song Regina had sung in last year's show. " 'When Irish eyes are smi-ling—' "

Matthew winged his smaller friend in the ribs. "You aren't high enough, man. 'When Irish eyes are smi-LING—' " His voice broke off in a screech.

"Want me to sing it again?" asked Regina. She didn't wait for an answer. " 'When EYE-rish eyes are smi-LEEEEEEEEENG—' "

Both boys clamped their hands over their ears and writhed in imitation agony. Regina grinned, imagining crystal goblets exploding all around her.

"Too bad you're going to miss the show," said Kate, settling beside her. "You're always something else."

Was that an insult or a compliment? That was the problem with Kate. You never knew.

"Who says I can't be in the show?" Regina said. "I'll figure out some way to get to the tryouts."

And Regina would. This was the year she was going to win the talent show. No matter that she had been in the show since first grade and had never won a prize.

Margaret twisted her ponytail, which was as long, thin, and yellow as a palomino horse's. Secretly, Regina coveted that hair. What she'd give to have hair that flowed in the wind when she ran! Her own wiry black bird's nest bobbed up and down like a Koosh ball. "You sure you can make the tryouts?" Margaret asked.

Regina smiled. It helped to have a a professional worrier as a best friend.

By the end of lunch, Regina had turned over all of her worrying to Margaret. In Music, she launched a fine, mellow belch. In P.E., she brushed her wiry black bangs, which were still loaded with gum, straight up like a troll's. She kept her eyes crossed for twenty minutes, earning her a dull headache but satisfying laughs in Social Studies. By the end of school, Regina had forgotten that she even had a problem. Regina the Great lived!

After detention, Regina raced through the warm April breeze to the family station wagon waiting by the curb. Regina's sisters called the car the Rust Bucket. The Rust Bucket wasn't *that* rusty, but it was the color of an old penny and not exactly sleek and fashionable. No matter. Mom and Dad were shopping for a new one.

"How was your day?" asked Mom, glancing at Regina in the rearview mirror.

"Can I have Margaret over?"

"Do you have homework?"

"No," said Regina, which was true. She had finished her work in detention hall. To Regina, speed was more important than correctness.

Mrs. Calhoun turned around to look at her daughter. "What happened to your hair?"

"I accidentally got gum in it."

Mom narrowed her eyes. "You get that gunk out— then you can call Margaret." She turned around and pulled out into the street.

The phone was ringing when they got in the door.

"Must be Margaret!" Regina sprinted to the phone.

4

It wasn't Margaret. It was her father.

"Regina, get your mother," Dad said.

"Where are you?"

Dad worked for Deskpro Electronics. He drove a nice white car his company gave him and stayed in all kinds of hotels. Regina collected the little wrapped soaps he brought home.

"Just get your mom." Her dad's voice sounded different. Low, almost shaky.

"Got any new soaps?"

"Regina, please." Now Dad just sounded tired. Not too tired, Regina hoped, to watch her perform a dance she'd made up when he got home.

"Mom," she yelled, holding the phone at arm's length. "Dad."

Mom took the phone. Meanwhile, Regina climbed up on the counter to get to the narrow cupboard above the refrigerator where Mom stashed cookies and snacks. It was an inconvenience, but it didn't stop Regina.

Armed with a bag of chocolate chip cookies, Regina hopped down from the counter. She was surprised to find her mother slumped against the desk by the phone.

"What's wrong, Mom?" She bit into a cookie.

Mom rubbed her temples. "Your dad," she said after a minute. "I've got to go get him."

"Why? Is his car broken?"

Mom's chin quivered, alarming Regina. "Is he sick?" Regina asked.

"I've got to go pick him up." Mom gulped as if she couldn't breathe. "Your father's just been fired."

## 2

# Snip!

Regina peered into the freezer, rubbing her tongue over her chipped tooth. Her stomach had begun hurting when Mom left to pick up Dad. Usually when her stomach ached, all she had to do was to eat. This time, six cookies hadn't done the job.

Don't be so dumb, she scolded herself. Dad was a Calhoun, and Calhouns always ended up on top.

She flipped open a carton of mocha almond fudge ice cream. Most of the ice cream had been scooped away, leaving the melted-and-refrozen crust on the sides. She clamped down the lid as the kitchen door flew open. Regina's sisters tromped into the kitchen.

"Don't tell me you didn't wear my navy cotton sweater," Maureen, the oldest one, yelled. "I can't find it, and I want to wear it tonight!"

"I didn't take it," sniffed Lydia. Though Lydia, fourteen, was a year younger than Maureen, she was the taller of the two. Since she liked to wear makeup, and Maureen hated it, she also looked older. Both girls, however, had their mother's smooth brown hair and brown eyes. Regina was the only one that got her dad's wiry black bird's nest.

Regina rifled through several Popsicle and frozen waffle boxes. All were empty. She and her sisters were famous for leaving empties in the freezer—for that matter, in the cupboards and in the fridge, too. It drove their mother crazy. She was thinking about throwing the boxes away, saving Mom a yell, when she was distracted by the Baggies in the freezer door.

"I know you're lying about my sweater," Maureen accused Lydia as Regina got out two of the five Baggies. "You know where it is."

"I do not," said Lydia. "I never wear your ugly clothes!"

"You do, too," said Maureen. "I've seen you in them. You always stink them up and stretch them out."

"I do not!"

While her sisters argued, Regina juggled the cold Baggies, admiring the crystalized grayish chunks inside. It was snow, from two winters ago. Though her mother wasn't crazy about keeping dirty snow in the freezer, Regina was glad she had saved it. There had been none this year.

That was the rotten thing about living in Atlanta. A whole winter could go by without snow on the ground. On the other hand, just one half-inch of good, sticking snow could close down every school in the city.

What a beautiful blizzard that storm of her fourth-grade year had been! A foot of snow covered everything. Every kid under the age of a hundred was outside playing.

Margaret had walked over in her dad's rubber fishing boots. They built snowmen and fended off Regina's sisters with snowballs until Dad came outside in his ancient letter jacket.

"I'll show you how a Calhoun makes an igloo," he said, stacking up blocks of rolled snow. "Give us a few minutes and we'll all be snug as a bug in a rug."

When they had finished the igloo and piled inside, Dad plugged the doorway and called for the Calhoun's yellow Labrador retriever, Bones, who was plowing through the snow with his snout. Bones usually slept all day in the den by the hot air vent, but to Regina's surprise, he bounded over and dug them out as determinedly as a trained rescue dog. Regina only wished she had a little keg to tie around his neck.

Now Bones' solid tail was thumping against Regina's legs. The sound of the freezer door had awakened him from his nap. Regina held the bags of snow away from his inquisitive nose while The Battle Of The Sisters raged around them.

"I'm giving you five seconds to come up with my sweater!" cried Maureen.

Lydia slammed her books down on the counter. "I don't have it!"

"Four seconds!"

Regina put the Baggies back in the freezer door. She found a strawberry yogurt in the refrigerator compartment, and trotted into the den, Bones following. She slung her legs over the arm of the flowered chair and began eating, turning up the volume of the TV when her sisters moved into the room.

"I'm not kidding, Lydia. Two seconds!"

There were other differences between Regina and her sisters besides age and hair color. Maureen and Lydia had nice, plain skin; she had five billion freckles. They had shiny brown eyes; she had muddy green. They were tall; she was extra puny. She got that from Dad, who was slightly thinner and shorter than Mom.

However, lack of size didn't stop Regina from wearing her sisters' clothes. She looked good in them! In fact, she had worn Maureen's navy sweater over her uniform to school on Tuesday. It was lying in a crumpled ball under her bed.

"Time's up, Lydia. Where's my sweater?"

Lydia pointed at Regina, who was suddenly interested in a commercial for toilet bowl cleanser. "She probably has it!"

"You better not have it!" Maureen declared. "Last time you stole my clothes, you spilled grape juice down the front of my new t-shirt."

"Communion wine," said Regina piously. Could she help it that there was a Mass on the last no-uniform day? She certainly hadn't meant to miss her lips with the communion cup.

"Regeeeena!" Maureen stalked toward her.

Regina could almost feel a wallop on her back. She had to throw Maureen off the scent, quick! "Dad got fired!"

Maureen froze in her tracks. "What?"

The looks on her sisters' faces made Regina's stomach thump. She ran her tongue over her tooth. "He got fired."

"When?" Maureen demanded.

"I don't know. A while ago. Mom went to pick him up."

"Where's his car?" asked Lydia.

"His car?" Maureen cried. "Don't you get it? They took it from him. He's not working anymore!"

Lydia sagged onto the couch. "What are we going to do about money?" she said, her voice wavering.

Regina plunked her yogurt cup on the floor, her appetite gone. Mom often joked that her part-time job at the pediatrician's office only brought home enough money to buy lunch. Regina ate a lot more than lunch. And what about clothes? Treats? A new car?

"Quit crying, both of you," Maureen ordered, looking dangerously close to sobbing herself. "If Dad comes home and sees you like that, he'll really feel bad."

"I'm not crying," Regina growled, rubbing her eyes with her shirt sleeve. Bones licked her elbow. Even he knew something was wrong.

Just then, Regina heard the rattling of the kitchen door. Lydia ran from the room.

*"Act happy,"* Maureen warned.

Regina's insides shriveled. She wanted to run like Lydia, but her bottom seemed glued to the chair.

Dad stalked into the den. He looked at his daughters and laughed. "Well, I can see you two have heard the news."

"What news?" said Regina.

Maureen flashed her a look of disgust. "Are you okay?" she asked Dad.

"I'll survive."

Maureen twisted the bottom of her t-shirt. "How'd it happen, Dad?"

Dad shook his head. "My boss was ordered to cut

10

half of his sales force—the company wasn't showing enough profit. I knew it was coming"—he sucked in his breath—"but I didn't think it'd be me."

Mom appeared behind him. "It wasn't his fault. Your dad is an excellent salesman." She pushed her hair off her forehead, closing her eyes for a moment. "Girls," she said when she opened them, "do you have homework?"

"Yes," said Maureen.

Before Regina could get out a proud "no," Dad said, "Ruth, do you need the car right now?"

"No," said Mom. "Where are you going?"

"To the unemployment office."

"Oh, Dan!" Mom cried. "You don't have to go there today! Take a nap. Take a walk. Baby yourself. Just don't go there, not yet."

"I want to get it over with." Dad noticed Regina sliding down in her chair. "Regina, I didn't die, you know."

"I know." Regina sat up. "Think you'll get a job real soon?"

The lines tightened around Dad's mouth. Regina felt Maureen's glare burning into her.

"Let's go, Ruth," said Dad. Maureen rushed from the room.

Regina hunched in her chair, working over her chipped tooth. How could Dad have lost his job? They had to have made a mistake at his work. Didn't they know who they were firing?

As soon as the kitchen door banged, Regina trudged to the bathroom. The suffering creature in the mirror seemed as strange and as distant as someone on TV. Her gaze wandered to the gum in her hair. She perked up.

Now *that* she could fix.

She rummaged through the bathroom drawer, remembering the last time she'd cut her hair. She'd been four. She had started out wondering if scissors cut hair as nicely as paper.

They did. Even more nicely.

When Mom had found her and quit screaming, she'd held Regina up to the mirror. Regina looked like she was wearing a flesh-colored swimming cap with a few tufts of hair glued on it.

Regina knew about scissors now. She'd cut off just a little hair. No problem.

She found the nail scissors under a box of Q-tips, then stretched out the first offending lock of gummy hair.

Snip!

Easy, baby.

# 3

# Kleenex Thief

Regina was modelling an evening gown/bath towel in the mirror when the phone rang.

"Regina!" Maureen yelled from her room.

Regina clutched the towel around herself and scampered to the phone in her parents' bedroom.

"Hello?"

"This is Margaret. What are you doing?"

"Taking a shower."

"A shower? Now?"

When her hair had turned out a little differently than she had expected, Regina thought a shampoo would help. "I felt dirty." Regina's tongue flicked over her tooth. She didn't like lying, especially to Margaret. "What are you doing?"

"Well, I was playing the piano."

"Oh." Regina paused. Should she tell Margaret about her dad?

"Regina, I've been thinking about your problem."

"My problem?" Regina caught her breath. How could Margaret know already?

"About missing the tryouts."

"Ohhhh."

"Regina, I've got the perfect solution for you."

"What?"

"Beg Mr. Amsden for forgiveness."

"He won't listen."

"Yes he will. Tell him that you're very sorry for chewing gum again in school, and that you'll do anything—clean his room, grade his papers, wash his car—*anything*—just as long as he lets you off during the tryouts."

Regina rubbed her tongue over her tooth, remembering another time she had begged somebody for forgiveness. It had been in Ms. Wilkie's class in kindergarten. Regina had discovered a cute little plastic-wrapped package of Kleenexes on the stove in the Play Kitchen. She soon observed that they were perfect for wiping the bottom of the dirty-faced doll she'd been mothering.

She was on the last Kleenex, still working on the doll bottom, when Janet Silver found her.

"Those are mine!" Janet screamed. "You stole them!"

"I didn't mean to!" Regina said. "I'm sorry."

Janet drew in her breath, winding up for maximum volume. "REGINA CALHOUN IS TOO POOR TO BUY KLEENEXES!"

The words cast an instant spell. Regina felt smaller, less smart, less wonderful. Regina the Great had shrunk into a tiny gray mouse.

Now a pinpoint hole of worry burned in her chest.

What would she do if her family actually did become poor?

Margaret's voice came over the line. "Regina?"

Maureen strolled by the bedroom door. She stopped and did a double-take. "What's with the little crew cut?"

Regina's hand went to her hair.

"Regina?" said Margaret. "You still there?"

"I've got to go. I'll call you later." Regina hung up. "Do you think it looks bad?" she asked Maureen. She ran her fingers over the prickly row of hair that used to be her bangs.

"Not if you're a female porcupine trying to attract a mate."

Regina followed Maureen into the bathroom. "What if I keep my hair brushed down like—"

"Regina!"

Regina whirled around. Her mother loomed cross-armed in the doorway.

"Regina, what have you done to your hair?"

"You just get home? Where's Dad?"

"Regina, it was cute to cut your hair when you were four. It is not cute now. When are you ever going to grow up?"

"I was just getting the gum out," said Regina, the fire spot growing in her chest. "You asked me to."

"I didn't ask you to mutilate yourself. Regina, I just can't handle this now." Mom's angry footsteps receded down the hall.

Regina pushed what was left of her bangs over her prickly patch. She'd only been doing what her mother had asked. She ran out of the bathroom, almost colliding with her father.

15

Dad grabbed her arms to set her straight, then trudged on wordlessly.

"Dad?" Regina's sore spot burned brighter. She darted after him. "Dad, did you bring me any soaps?"

"What?" Dad plodded into his room, not waiting for a reply.

Regina followed. "Any soaps?" she asked, hopping onto the bed next to his suitcase.

Dad opened his suitcase and reached into a side pocket. "Here. Two Holiday Inns, three Ramadas." He stared at the bed, rubbing the back of his neck.

"How many states you been in this week?"

Dad didn't answer.

"Want to see me do a dance?"

No answer.

"I know"—Regina watched his face—"how about playing me a game of backgammon?"

Dad's gaze remained on the bed.

Regina stared at her father. He usually *begged* her to play backgammon. He won every time. "Calhouns love to win!" he'd crow when he tromped her.

The phone rang again. Dad lunged for the receiver by his bed.

"Hello?" His face fell. "It's for you," he said, handing Regina the phone.

Now Regina's entire heart felt like a shimmering ember. "I'll take it in the kitchen."

She plodded out to the phone on the kitchen wall. "Hello?"

"Regina, it's me again, Margaret."

"Oh, hi, Margaret."

"Is something wrong?"

Regina almost smiled. When it came to worrying, Margaret had antennae. "No."

"I wanted to tell you, Kate called me."

"What'd *she* want?"

"Regina, she's trying out for the talent show."

"Is that all? Who cares? She sings like a cow with a toothache."

"She's not singing this year."

"She's not?"

"She's dancing."

"That's what I'm doing!"

"I know," said Margaret, "and Kate's been taking jazz lessons. She's using the steps her class learned for a production of 'West Side Story'."

"That old thing?" Regina sought out her tooth. She'd never taken a dance lesson in her life.

Maureen stomped into the kitchen. "Regina, get off the phone. I want to use it."

Lydia appeared behind her, nose and eyes red. "Then I get to use it," she said, sniffing.

"Got to go," Regina said into the phone.

"Practice your dancing," said Margaret.

"I will." Regina hung up.

Lydia dabbed at her eyes, then froze. "What'd you do to your hair?"

"Charming, isn't it?" said Maureen.

Regina slipped by without a comment. She had plenty of troubles without worrying about a few short hairs.

She locked herself in the bathroom and looked in the mirror. A girl with her dad's black bird's nest glared back at her.

She'd figure out a way of beating Kate. She had to. She was a Calhoun! And Calhouns loved to win.

❀ ❀ ❀

# 4

# *Cut the Craziness*

The next morning, Regina stopped doodling behind her binder as kids poured into the classroom. "Well?" she asked, giving Margaret one last peek. "What do you think?"

"Your hair's not *that* bad," Margaret said.

"It's not?"

"I've seen worse." Margaret studied her closely, arms crossed. "Who's that singer who shaved off all her hair?"

"Margaret!"

"Not that you look like her! You always look cute."

Regina frowned. Margaret would say that if Regina had pepper stuck between her teeth.

Just then, Arley and Matthew bounded into the room biffing each other on the arm, Matthew towering above his smaller friend.

"Hide me!" Regina yelped.

Margaret jumped in front of Regina's desk, just as Arley gave Matthew a shove into Margaret.

"Quit it!" Matthew yelled, his bread-loaf–sized oxfords thudding as he stumbled forward. He untangled himself from a pink-faced Margaret. "Arley wants to ask you girls something, only he's too chicken to ask you himself."

Behind her binder, Regina perked up. Arley had given her presents on Christmas, Valentine's Day, and her birthday since second grade. He threw pickles in her milk at lunch. He loved her.

"I guess Regina's not interested," said Matthew. "We'll just have to ask someone else."

"What?" Regina cried, leaning around Margaret. "What do you want to know?"

Arley's mouth dropped open as if yanked by an invisible string. "What happened to your hair?"

Regina's hand went to her bald spot.

Matthew snickered. "What'd you do, run into Mr. Kraus? You look like you've got a janitor's broom stuck on your head."

"Yeah? Well, guess what? I can smell your breath clear over here." She glanced at Arley, expecting a laugh, but Arley only tossed his curtain of hair, frowning.

Matthew blew into his giant-sized hands, then, realizing Regina was watching, stopped. "You Broom Brain!"

"Stink Breath!"

Regina flashed Arley a grin. *Come on, laugh.*

Chairs scraped against the floor as kids around them

took their seats. The pencil sharpener ground. Arley gazed towards his desk.

Confusion beat in Regina's stomach like a trapped bird. "So what did you want to ask us?"

"Ask 'em, Romeo," said Matthew, slugging Arley in the arm.

Arley looked down at his shoes as if surprised to find they were there.

"Okay, chicken," Matthew said, shifting on his black bread loaves. "I'll ask them. You uglies want to race us at recess today?"

Regina pulled her gaze away from Arley. "We've already raced you. Last fall. I won."

"She did," Margaret agreed.

"She did not," said Matthew. "She fell. We want a rematch."

"What makes you ready to run all of a sudden?" Regina asked, directing her question at Arley.

"We've felt sorry for you long enough," said Matthew.

Arley said nothing.

"Okay, you're on," Regina barked, "but be ready to lose." Arley turned on his heel and headed for his desk.

"Hey, Arley," she called after him, "see you at recess, slowpoke!"

Arley opened his Vocabulary book. Vocabulary class wasn't until after Math and English. And Regina knew Arley hated Vocabulary.

Later, at lunch, Margaret pulled her sandwich out of a Baggie. "I'm glad we didn't have to race them at recess."

Regina peered at the window on the far side of the

20

lunchroom. Rain streamed down the glass behind where Arley and Matthew sat with Teresa Corvi and her friends. "They were lucky. We would have pounded 'em."

"Maybe *you* would have. They would have beaten me."

Regina shook her head. Margaret was almost as fast as she was. She could at least have beaten Matthew. Margaret just didn't believe in herself. Regina couldn't understand how anyone could not believe in herself. If you didn't think you could do something, who would?

Kate set her lunch tray next to Margaret's. "Where are Arley and Matthew?"

"Who knows?" said Regina. "Who cares?"

"She thinks they were afraid she'd beat them in a race," Margaret said.

"That shouldn't be a problem," said Kate, sitting down. "When you get near the finish line, Regina, just flash them your bald spot. That'll stop 'em."

Margaret cut Regina a troubled look, then bit into her sandwich.

Regina scowled at her potato chips. Why did Margaret like Kate? Just because they had been friends since kindergarten—what a crummy reason. Couldn't Margaret see that Kate was always getting in the way?

"Look," said Kate. She nodded across the lunchroom towards the boys.

Regina peered over her shoulder just as Arley dropped a pickle into Teresa Corvi's milk. Teresa screamed and pulled on Arley's sleeve.

"Isn't that what he used to do to your milk?" said Kate.

"Don't worry," said Margaret, "he still likes you."

21

Regina caught her breath. If Margaret had to say it, then it probably wasn't true.

"Why don't you go over there and get him?" said Kate. "Ask him why he doesn't love you anymore."

Regina gave Kate a cold stare. Just because Regina wanted to do that very thing didn't mean Kate should say it.

Kate put her paper napkin on her lap. "Did Amsden let you out of the detention yet?"

Regina looked over her shoulder at Mr. Amsden, who was sitting at the teacher's table, eating cottage cheese out of a Tupperware container. "Not yet."

She glanced back at Arley. He now had the lid off the salt shaker and was pouring salt into Teresa's milk while Teresa pounded him on the head.

Regina jumped up. If she had to sit and watch Arley destroy someone else's drink for one more second, she was going to burst.

She marched over to Mr. Amsden's table. "Please, Mr. Amsden," she begged over the lunchroom roar. "Please let me out of detention today. I promise I'll serve it next Monday!"

Mr. Amsden looked up from a conversation he was having with Miss Sparks, the P.E. teacher. "Hello, Regina," he said, dabbing his mouth with his napkin. "Having a nice lunch?"

Back at their table, a worried look rumpled the skin between Margaret's eyes. Regina kept going.

"I want to go to the tryouts. I *need* to go to the tryouts. Please let me out of detention! Please!"

Mr. Amsden stood up. "Come on, Regina. Cut the craziness."

Across the cafeteria, Arley opened the pepper shaker.

22

Regina dropped to her knees. "You want me to beg? I'll beg. Please, Mr. Amsden, please, please, please, please, please!"

"Get up, Regina!" Mr. Amsden frowned at Miss Sparks.

"Not until you say I can serve my detention later!" cried Regina, scuttling after him. Her knees stuck to the dirty floor, reducing her speed.

Mr. Amsden stepped out of her reach. "Regina, if it were anyone else, I'd waive the detention. But with your history—I have to say no. Even if you beg."

"But I want to win!" said Regina, hating Arley, who at that moment was stirring Teresa's drink with a straw. "I need to win!"

"Well, you can't win down there," said Mr. Amsden. Miss Sparks chuckled.

Regina staggered to her feet. For once in her life, she didn't appreciate a laugh.

"Don't worry," Margaret said after Regina trudged back to their table. "You can come to tryouts late."

"Sure," Regina said, picking mournfully at a piece of black goo on her knee.

A clapping resounded from across the lunchroom. Regina looked up, heart thumping. *Arley?*

"Bravo, Broom Brain!" Matthew leaned back in his seat, applauding. "Kraus won't need to mop the floor now that you cleaned it with your knees."

"Oh, be quiet, Stink Breath!" Regina muttered. She took a sip of her milk, the first time she'd been able to this year. It went down like vinegar.

23

# 5

# Knock 'Em Dead

Mr. Amsden looked at the watch cutting into his pudgy arm. "Okay, Regina. Time."

"Yay!" Regina hopped up from her seat, the only kid in detention.

"Knock 'em dead!" Mr. Amsden called as she raced from the room.

Regina smelled the cafeteria before she came to it: old peas. She burst through the doorway.

Except for Mr. Kraus putting away chairs, the cafeteria was empty.

Regina's heart stopped. "Where's the tryouts?" she yelled to Mr. Kraus.

"They're over." Mr. Kraus ran his arm across his mustache, then went back to work.

Regina backed away. No. The tryouts couldn't have ended yet!

She ran to the office. "Where is everybody?" she cried to Mrs. Greenway, the school secretary.

Mrs. Greenway poked a manila envelope into one of the teacher mailboxes. "Regina, what'd you do to your hair?"

Regina frowned. Why was everyone making such a big deal over her hair? "Did Mrs. Demetroff leave?" Mrs. Demetroff, the music teacher, ran the talent show.

Just then the principal, Mrs. Yoder, strolled out of her office. "Another detention, Regina?" she asked.

Regina scowled. Mr. Amsden had sent her down to Mrs. Yoder's office for a "chat" earlier in the year. Mrs. Yoder said if they had to do any more "chatting," Regina's parents would be asked to come join the conversation.

"I believe Regina's interested in the tryouts," said Mrs. Greenway, stuffing more envelopes into the mailboxes.

"The talent show just might be the place for you to burn off some of that excess energy, Regina," said Mrs. Yoder, "but Mrs. Demetroff had to wrap up the tryouts early. Her son is ill."

"Did they finish?"

"I think so. Anyhow, you just missed her. Regina, whatever prompted you to cut your—"

"Excuse me!" Regina darted from the office. Maybe she could still catch Mrs. Demetroff.

Regina's legs pumped like pistons. She could outrun a horse! If only Arley could see her.

She peeled around the corner of the school and beheld a miracle. Mrs. Demetroff was in the teacher's parking lot, loading boxes into the trunk of her car.

"Mrs. Demetroff! Mrs. Demetroff!"

25

Mrs. Demetroff looked up. Just then, Margaret jogged around from the other side of the car, carrying a box of books. Another miracle!

"Hey, everyone—I'm done!"

Before Margaret could congratulate her, Kate followed, toting her own box. "So the convict escaped."

Regina dropped to a walk.

"Missed you at the tryouts, Regina." Mrs. Demetroff brushed a blonde wing of hair from her eyes. "I had to leave early. My son's sick."

"I told Mrs. Demetroff you wanted to come," Margaret said, handing Mrs. Demetroff her box.

"Too bad," said Kate, casting Regina a superior smile as she gave Mrs. Demetroff her container. "Too late."

Mrs. Demetroff stowed both boxes in the trunk. "Thanks, girls, you're a lifesaver. I'm in a huge hurry."

"Maybe you can have a makeup tryout," Margaret suggested as Mrs. Demetroff got in her car. "For people who couldn't come."

"I'll have to think about it." Mrs. Demetroff shut her door with a thunk.

Regina gasped. This was the year she was going to win! What if Mrs. Demetroff decided against having a makeup?

"Wait!" she shouted through Mrs. Demetroff's window. "I'll show you my act right now!"

Regina whirled into her routine. She cartwheeled and back-bended on the asphalt of the parking lot, ignoring the little pebbles biting the palms of her hands, disregarding her lack of P.E. shorts under the skirt of her uniform. Surely Mrs. Demetroff had seen underwear before. And Regina had on her good ones.

Mrs. Demetroff rolled down her electric window. "I think I get the idea, Regina. I'll announce who made it on Monday." She rolled up the window and put the car in reverse.

" 'Bye, Mrs. Demetroff!" Regina yelled, cartwheeling after the car as it pulled away. She slammed herself into the splits.

"Regina," said Margaret, "there's your mom."

The Rust Bucket rested at the curb in front of the cafeteria entrance.

Regina eased herself to her feet. "Anyone need a ride?" she asked, gingerly brushing the gravel from her thighs.

Margaret shook her head, looking guilty. "Kate already offered me one."

"Oh."

"But I can go with you next time," Margaret said.

Just then, a red convertible streaked into the parking lot, the driver's turquoise scarf whipping in the wind. When Kate waved her arms, the car came purring towards them.

"Hi, Mom."

Kate's mother tipped down her sunglasses, though Regina would have recognized Mrs. Glendenning with them on. Everyone in town knew Liz Glendenning. She did the six o'clock news on Channel Four. "Get in, Kate," said Mrs. Glendenning, "I'm in a hurry."

"Come on, Margaret," said Kate, climbing onto the white leather of the back seat.

Regina watched her best friend zoom away with Kate, Margaret's palomino ponytail flying straight back, Kate's brown bob flapping. Regina plodded over to the

Rust Bucket and scooted onto the patched vinyl back seat. Curled edges of gray duct tape stuck to her legs.

She glimpsed a wiry black bird's nest like her own. "Dad!"

"Surprise you?"

Regina nodded.

"Well, today I just happen to be free. I hope you won't have a chance to get used to it."

Regina shifted her legs to unstick them from the duct tape as the station wagon turned into the street. "When are you getting another job?" she asked.

Dad snorted. "If I knew that, I wouldn't be losing sleep at night, would I?"

"Oh, Dad," said Regina, "you'll get a job. You're smart."

"Smart has nothing to do with it. For every one job, there's a hundred people trying to land it. If someone comes along with more education or experience, then they'll get hired, not me."

"You have a lot of education and experience." Regina's tongue sought out her chipped tooth. "Don't you?"

Dad glanced in the rearview mirror. "Hey, don't worry about it."

"I'm not worried."

Why was Dad talking like this? Not only was he smart, he was handsome. She looked just like him! He was winner—a Calhoun!

"Do you have any homework?" Dad asked.

"No," said Regina, not really hearing his question. All those other dads with education and experience had better watch out. Her dad was going to tromp them all, easy as playing backgammon.

28

# 6

# À Cinderella Story

"Take off your shoes," said Dad when they got inside the kitchen door.

"Why?"

"Don't look at me like that. I just shampooed the carpet."

"All right." Regina slipped off her sneakers.

"Put them by the door, please."

Regina lifted her brows, but put her shoes in place. She climbed up on the counter by the refrigerator and reached for a box of cookies in the overhead cabinet.

"Make sure you don't get crumbs on the floor. I just mopped it."

Regina hauled the cookies down to the counter.

"And put the box away when you're done."

Regina stared at her dad. "Now when are you getting a job?"

Dad snorted. "I'm just helping your mother since you kids can't seem to fit it into your busy schedules. Take a look in the fridge."

Regina opened the refrigerator. A few items sat in orderly rows on clean shelves. The empty bottles and containers were gone.

She gasped. Her snow! She flung open the freezer. Though all of the empty wrappers were gone, and only a box of frozen spinach and a loaf of bread hunkered in the swirls of cold air, the five Baggies of gray ice were still in the door.

"Don't worry, Regina," said Dad, "I wouldn't throw out your snow."

Regina sighed with relief, then bit into one of her cookies.

"So, how was school today?" asked Dad, watching her eat.

"Great," she said with a full mouth.

Dad leaned against the counter. Unlike Mom, who made a lot of noise about not making a mess but didn't stick around for the clean-up, he watched her eat as if daring the crumbs to fall.

Regina took one more hestitant bite, then shoved the last two cookies in her mouth. She scooted into the family room. Bones greeted her with a tail thump from his place by the air-conditioning vent.

Dad trailed behind Regina, setting off a new round of tail-thumps from Bones. "Do you have any detentions next week, Regina?"

"Yes." Regina squirmed under his gaze. "But only until Friday."

"Regina, I'm not going to put up with that."

Regina made a show of looking around the room. "Where are Maureen and Lydia?"

"Cleaning their rooms. Like you're going to do—" he checked his watch "—in about two minutes."

"I am?" Regina made a face. She liked her room messy. Fortunately, so did Maureen, with whom she shared space. Unfortunately, a person couldn't walk inside their door without crunching something underfoot.

"Yep, you are." Dad settled into his recliner and clicked on the TV with the remote control.

"Where's Mom?"

"She's at work. Vickie took her." Vickie was a nurse at the pediatrician's office where Mom worked.

Dad flipped to a baseball game.

"Oh, look," said Regina. "The Braves."

Dad's gaze strayed from Regina to the TV.

"Maddux's pitching, Dad."

Dad nodded, not looking back at her.

Regina stifled a sigh of relief. Now she could get more cookies and eat them in peace.

The phone rang. Dad bolted upright.

"Regina!" came Maureen's voice from the back of the house.

Dad sagged in his recliner.

Regina trotted to the phone in the kitchen. "Hello?"

"Hi, it's Margaret."

Regina frowned. "How was your car ride?"

There was a short silence on the other end of the line. "Regina, I would have rather have gone with you, but Kate had already asked me."

"Oh, I don't care."

Another short silence. "Well, anyway, it wasn't that fun. Kate's mom made us listen to oldies—the *Eagles*—

31

gross!—loud. Your mom always lets us listen to 98 Rock."

Regina smiled. Nice try, Margaret. She rubbed her hand over her ex-bangs. They felt like the short fur on the top of Bones' head. "Was Arley at the tryouts?"

"No . . ."

"No, but what?"

Margaret's sigh shuddered over the phone line. "You aren't going to like this, Regina."

"Like what?"

"Teresa Corvi was there."

"Oh, I don't care about her. What was she doing, another one of her stupid tap dance routines? How many years is she going to wear that dumb sailor suit?"

"Not this year."

"She's not?"

"She's doing a jazz routine."

"Big deal! So is Kate. So is everybody. I bet nobody does good walkovers."

"Regina, she has strobe lights."

"Strobe lights?"

"You know—those lights that flash real fast and make everything look jerky?"

"I know what strobe lights are." Regina scrambled on top of the counter by the refrigerator, stretching the phone cord to its limit.

Margaret heaved another sigh. "That's not the worst part."

Regina snagged the cookie box by the tips of her fingers, and clutching it like a security blanket, hopped down from the counter. "Yeah?"

"You know that necklace Arley wears that he made out of little bitty beads?"

32

Regina fumbled with the wrapper around the tray of cookies. Her fingers had become as thick and rubbery as erasers. She fought with the paper, tearing it.

"Teresa's wearing it."

Bang! The cookies fell.

Mom stepped in the kitchen door just as two cookies rolled by like wagonwheels. "Regina!" she shouted. "What are you doing?" She marched to the utility closet at the end of the kitchen.

Dad flew in from the family room. "Don't clean that up for her, Ruth. She's capable."

Regina slumped against the counter. Teresa Corvi was wearing Arley's beads.

"Hang up, Regina!" said Mom.

Regina managed to move her mouth. "Margaret, I've got to go."

"Regina, it's probably not what it looks like," said Margaret. "Maybe Teresa forced him to give it to her. Maybe she got a necklace just like his. You don't know, maybe—"

"Thanks, Margaret. I'll call you later."

Regina hung up the phone, hurt building in her chest like pressure in a shaken soda can.

"Sweep," Dad ordered. "And when I come back, that mess better be perfectly cleaned up, young lady."

"Honestly, Regina." Mom picked up the mail from the kitchen counter and followed Dad to the family room.

Regina dragged to the utility closet. What was so great about strobe lights, anyhow? It was a talent show, not a light show.

She got out the broom and dustpan, imagining herself in rags and a kerchief. She pretended she was in a cot-

33

tage, sweeping the fireplace, while in the background her parents yelled, *Cinderella!*

She saw Teresa Corvi jamming her foot into a glass slipper held by Arley. "What's wrong with the shoe?" Teresa yelled. "It won't fit! There's something wrong with it!"

Arley tried the slipper on Regina. Regina's foot glided inside like a hand into a silk glove.

"It fits!" cried Arley. "And it stinks!"

"I love you, too!" said Regina, squeezing him like a teddy bear.

"REGINA?" came Dad's voice from the family room. "I DON'T HEAR ANY ACTION!"

The wonderful scene faded.

"REGINA? ARE YOU SWEEPING?"

Regina swept, her broom a regular broom; her school uniform, the usual. She was an average girl with a chipped tooth and no boy to give her presents.

Somehow, she had to fix that.

❀   ❀   ❀

# 7

# Making Adjustments

Later, after sweeping a tidy pile of cookie crumbs under
the rug by the sink, Regina wandered into the family
room.

"Well," Mom was saying to Dad, who stood over
her at the desk, "then I guess we'll have to drop it
this year."

"Drop what?" asked Regina, flopping into the flowered chair.

Mom and Dad stiffened. "Did you clean up the
kitchen?" asked Dad.

"Yes. Drop what, Mom?"

"Nothing." Mom shuffled some of the opened envelopes on the desks. "Nothing."

Dad ran his fingers through his bird's nest. "We
ought to go ahead and tell her, Ruth. We might as well
get used to it."

"Get used to what?" Regina's tongue went for her chipped tooth.

Dad and Mom exchanged a look. "Making adjustments," said Dad.

"What adjustments?"

"Well, with me not working—"

"You're going to work!" Regina broke in.

"Thanks for your vote of confidence, Regina," said Dad. "I wish things were that simple. But the truth of the matter is, I might not find another job for a long time."

"Oh yes, you are! I know you are!"

Dad cleared his throat. "Even so, in the meantime, we're going to have to cut back on some things."

"What things?" Something tightened in Regina's chest.

Dad looked at Mom. Mom laid the envelopes on the table by the couch. "For starters, the Pool Club membership," she said.

"It won't be forever," Dad said, "just until I get my feet on the ground. Who knows? Maybe we'll be able to pick it up in July or August."

Regina hopped up. "But the pool opens in three weeks! What about my friends? What about swim team? What am I going to do all summer?"

"Oh, Regina, it's not that bad," said Dad. "We can go swimming at Lake Lanier."

"Lake Lanier? Who wants to swim in brown water with fish biting at their toes?"

Her parents exchanged a grim expression, causing icy fingers of fear to glide up her spine. They were really serious.

"Never mind," she said, backing from the room.

36

"I'll just play in the hose this summer. Who needs the dumb old Pool Club, anyhow?" She ran before her parents could say anything more.

Regina blasted into her room. Maureen lifted up one of the earphones to her Diskman. "My side's already clean, Regina. Don't mess it up."

Regina threw herself onto her own bed.

Maureen lowered her earphones to her neck and laid down her book. "Something wrong?"

"No."

"Come on. You look like you did when Mom told you that you couldn't keep a horse in the garage."

Regina scowled. She'd had that all worked out. She could have made a nice place for the horse next to the car. She would have ridden it in the back yard, around and around the dogwood tree. However, that wasn't the problem now. The problem was that she could see herself slumped outside the Pool Club fence, a pitiful outcast, while her friends splashed in the pool.

"Or," said Maureen, "let me guess—you want to build more rabbit traps and Mom told you to stop wasting cardboard boxes."

Regina glared at her sister. Someday, when a rabbit did venture into one of the boxes she had rigged open with a stick, she wouldn't let Maureen give it one single pat. "Just be quiet, would you?"

"Okay." Maureen snapped her headphones over her ears.

Regina rolled onto her back, her troubles washing over her in waves. No job, no pool. . . . No Arley.

How could he give Teresa his beads? Teresa never played The Star Spangled Banner by blowing on her arm. Teresa never stood on top of her desk when the teacher left the room. When Mr. Amsden tried to quiet the classroom by saying, "I hear voices!" Teresa never replied, "I hear voices, too!"

Regina choked down the lump rising in her throat. Maybe Margaret was right. Maybe there was a logical explanation.

She sat up. She could find out, now.

She reached for the phone between the beds, peeking at Maureen out of the corner of her eye.

Maureen turned a page of her book, head bobbing.

Regina dialed.

"Hello?"

For a second, Regina couldn't speak. Arley's voice was so cute it took her wind away. She glanced at Maureen. Still reading. "Arley?"

"Oh. Hi."

Regina gasped. Three years of devotion, and all she got was *Oh, hi?*

She forced a laugh. "Did you see Robbie Colberg at recess today?"

"No."

"He was chasing Margaret and me all over the parking lot. He thought we were running from him because he was acting like a vampire, but that wasn't it at all. He had this great big booger on his cheek!"

Arley's end of the line was silent. Perhaps he hadn't understood.

"Here was this big huge greenie," Regina explained, "and everytime we screamed, he thought it was because he was saying 'I vant to suck your blood!' "

More silence.

Anger boiled up in Regina's chest. She glared at the teddy bear he had given her for Valentine's Day sitting

38

amongst the junk on the top of her dresser. "You want your bear back or not?"

There was a pause, and then, "I don't care."

"Well! Then I don't care either! I think I'll throw it down the garbage disposal."

"Who are you yelling at?" Maureen said, pulling an earphone away from her head.

"Nobody!" Regina screamed. Into the phone she yelled, "And I didn't want your ugly beads, either!" She slammed down the receiver.

"Who was that?" asked Maureen.

Regina snatched up the phone and dialed, breathing hard. Matthew answered immediately.

"Matthew?"

"Oh, hi."

"Why is everybody saying, 'oh, hi' these days! Why can't they say, 'Regina—hello!' or 'Regina—good to hear you!' "

"Regina—good to hear the Broom Brain."

"Tell me *now,*" Regina demanded. "Why doesn't Arley like me anymore?"

There was a brief pause. "You really want to know?"

Regina's heart stopped. She hadn't expected an affirmative answer. "Y-yes."

"I guess he doesn't like your fuzz head."

"That couldn't be it!" Regina cried. "Hair grows!"

"You asked me—I told you. Hey, did you see that boog on Colberg's cheek at recess today?"

Regina banged down the phone. She stomped over to Arley's teddy bear, and with all her furious might, yanked an arm and a leg in opposite directions.

Maureen flipped up an earphone. "What are you doing? You're going to rip that thing."

"Good! I hate it!"

Maureen squinted her eyes. "Arley drop you or what?"

The words seared Regina's ears like a branding iron. She jerked on the bear's limbs.

"Give the bear a break, Goof. Forget Arley."

"I can't!"

"You can." Maureen snapped back her earphone. "Get over it."

Regina couldn't get over it! It wasn't so much that she had lost Arley, it was that he had lost her. She, the hilarious Regina Calhoun, dropped!

She heaved the bear across the room. Its nose made a satisfying click as it hit the wall. She dialed the phone.

"Mrs. Goodman, is Margaret there?"

"I'm afraid not," said Margaret's mother. "Someone from Channel Four just came by and picked her up. She and Kate are going to watch Liz Glendenning tape tonight's show."

"Oh . . . Thanks." Regina hung up and sank on the bed. She needed Margaret. She couldn't worry about Arley and Teresa alone.

⌘     ⌘     ⌘

*8*

# Fred Astaire's No Dummy

The next morning, Regina dialed Margaret's number before turning on the Saturday cartoons.

"Mrs. Goodman," said Regina, wrapping herself in the kitchen phone cord, "is Margaret there?"

"Not yet, Regina. She spent the night at Kate's. Do you want her to call you when she gets home?"

Regina unwound slowly out of the cord. "That's okay. No thanks."

"Dad and I are going to the Petersons," Mom announced, walking into the kitchen with Dad as Regina hung up the phone. "Mr. Peterson thinks he might have a job for your dad with his company."

Dad straightened his tie. "How do I look?"

"Great," said Regina.

"You don't have to worry about what you look like, Dan," said Mom. "Roy Peterson's an old friend."

Regina waved as they left, picturing herself skipping between shiny new cars on a car lot. This might be a good day after all.

Maureen slouched into the kitchen in a droopy t-shirt and boxers, her hair still tangled from sleep. "Mom and Dad leave?"

"Yes," said Regina. "Dad's going to get a new job."

"Really?" Maureen's puffy eyes opened wider.

"Yep. Then we're getting a new car."

"Dream on." Maureen got out a bagel and sawed it in half before cramming it down the toaster.

Regina poured herself some Cheerios. "Hey, Maureen, do we have any strobe lights around here?"

"What do you want a strobe for?"

Regina kicked a handful of fallen Cheerios under the counter. "My dance routine."

"All we've got are flashlights. You can shake a couple of them up and down."

"Ha, ha."

Maureen leaned against the counter, waiting for her bagel to toast. "I know, Goof—why don't you darken the room and hold a flashlight under your lip while you do your routine? You can be a dancing monster."

"Who's a monster?" asked Lydia, walking into the kitchen with her hair up in a towel and holding out freshly painted nails.

"Regina," said Maureen.

"What's new."

A burning smell filled the kitchen.

"Got any other ideas?" Regina asked.

Maureen fished most of her bagel out of the toaster, then scraped the burnt part into the sink. "The goof's trying to think up a way to spice up her dance routine."

"The best dance I ever saw," said Lydia, pulling a pitcher of orange juice out of the fridge, fingers splayed, "was in that old movie that's always on at Christmas. *Holiday Inn* I think it is. That famous dancing guy is in it—what's his name?"

"Fred Astaire," said Maureen.

"That's him." Lydia poured the juice into a glass, pausing long enough to check the condition of her nails. "Remember the dance he does with the firecrackers?"

"I do!" Regina cried. "He lights little firecrackers and throws them at his feet while he's tap dancing."

"Right," said Lydia. "Now that is a cool routine."

"Do we have any firecrackers?" Regina asked.

Lydia stopped sipping her juice. "You can't be serious."

"We don't have any," said Maureen. "Besides, I think firecrackers are illegal in Georgia." She bit into her bagel. Brown crumbs sprinkled to the floor.

"Even if they weren't illegal and we did have some, what would you light them with?" Lydia said. "In *Holiday Inn,* Fred Astaire lit them with a cigarette he was smoking."

Regina frowned. She was sorry that firecrackers were illegal, but a little pack of tiny firecrackers didn't seem so dangerous. She'd seen the remainders of them in the Pool Club parking lot the morning after the Fourth of July. But no matter how much she wanted to win the contest, she wasn't going to smoke. Cigarettes stank.

"Forget it, Regina," Maureen said around a mouthful of bagel.

Lydia sipped at her juice. "Really. Don't get any of your wild ideas."

43

"Oh, don't worry." Regina's tongue flicked against her tooth.

The phone rang. Maureen answered, then held out the receiver to Regina. "For you, Porcupine."

"Hi, Regina," said Margaret.

Regina remembered where Margaret had spent the night. "Oh, hi."

"What are you doing?"

Regina made her voice as chilly as possible. "Nothing."

"Sorry I couldn't call you sooner. I was at Kate's. I wanted to go home a long time ago, but her mom wouldn't get up. I had to call my mom to come get me."

"You mean Kate's mom sleeps later than a kid? It's almost ten-thirty."

"I guess she's tired. After her eleven o'clock show, she went to a party."

Regina supposed it must be true. Margaret never lied.

"Can you come over?" asked Margaret.

Regina perked up. "When?"

"In about an hour. I've got to practice my piano first."

Margaret hoped to play the piano in the talent show, performing a song she had written herself. She was good, Regina thought, but even old Mozart himself couldn't make piano playing exciting. Maybe she could lend Margaret some firecrackers to set off at the end of her song . . .

"Are you coming?" Margaret asked.

"My parents are at their friends' house," said Regina. "As soon as they get home, I'll call you."

44

But Regina's parents didn't get home until dinnertime.

"Did you get a job?" Regina asked when Mr. and Mrs. Calhoun walked into the family room where the girls were watching TV.

"I don't know yet," said Dad.

"Mr. Peterson is looking for something for him," said Mom.

"Couldn't Mr. Peterson have told you that in less than seven hours?" Regina exclaimed. "I was supposed to go over to Margaret's."

"Too late for that," said Mom. "Maybe tomorrow."

But the girls couldn't get together the next day. Church blew the morning, then in the afternoon, Regina's mother made her go with her to Aunt Arlene's house.

Monday, however, was a better day. As soon as Dad dropped Regina off at school in the Rust Bucket, she ran to the bulletin board in front of the office. Sure enough, her name was on the list of people who had made it into the talent show.

"Congratulations," said Kate, coming up behind her.

Regina scanned the names. "You made it, too. Good going," she said half-heartedly.

"Oh, look. Margaret got in."

"Of course," Regina sniffed.

"I see Teresa made it. Did you hear about her strobe lights?"

"Yes. Big deal."

"That's what I say. Gimmicks aren't everything. Teresa can't even dance."

"I know." Regina shifted uncomfortably. It wasn't her custom to agree with Kate.

"I think gimmicks are dumb, don't you?"

"Well . . ." Regina's tongue flicked over her tooth. A gimmick was only dumb when it wasn't the greatest.

"Hey, Broom Brain!" shouted Matthew, trotting past with Arley.

"Shut up, Stink Breath," said Regina, her gaze zooming in on Arley's neck, which had turned red.

The beads were gone.

"Come on, Kate," she blurted, "let's go."

Kate's eyebrows rose in surprise. "Me?"

Regina marched away, not waiting for Kate. Fred Astaire was no dummy, and neither was she. She'd figure out how to duplicate his firecracker routine if it killed her. Then, when she won the talent show, would she give Arley the time of day?

No way, baby!

✺    ✺    ✺

# 9

# Black Cats

That night, Regina sat on the arm of Dad's recliner as he looked through the "help wanted" ads in the newspaper.

"There's nothing in here," he muttered, dropping the newspaper in his lap. He drew in a breath. "Want do you want, Regina?"

"Dad, do you have any firecrackers?"

"Firecrackers? What for?"

"A—a school project."

"Firecrackers, in school? I thought they were illegal in Georgia."

"Not the little bitty ones."

"Oh, really?" One of Dad's brows shot towards his bird's nest. "Well, I did get some Black Cats in Tennessee on one of my trips a couple of years ago. In some place called Crazy Larry's."

"One of those places with all the flashing lights and

47

lit-up Ferris Wheels? You went in one without me? Dad!''

"I had to use the restroom. Anyhow, I never got around to breaking out the firecrackers. Forgot about them. They're probably all duds now.''

"What kind were they?''

"Black Cats. They come in a package about yay big.'' He made an oblong with his fingers the size of a baseball card.

Regina's heart raced. "Where'd you put them?''

"I don't know. In my closet somewhere. Forget about them, Regina. They're no good anymore.'' Dad stretched his arms behind his head. "How do you feel about playing your old man in some backgammon?''

Just then, Bones got stiff-leggedly to his feet. He nudged the patio door with his nose and wagged his tail.

"Oh, look, Dad, Bones wants out. I'll get him.'' Regina hopped off Dad's chair to let the dog outside, then skipped towards the hall . . . and Dad's closet.

"Regina, where you going?'' Dad called after her.

"To my room,'' she sang out, adding in her head, *first*.

The next day at lunch, Margaret beamed as she put her tray down between Regina's and Kate's. "Did you see Arley just now?''

"No,'' said Regina pointedly. She had been going out of her way to avoid Arley since yesterday. The plan was to make him miss her.

"He's got his beads back on!''

Arley was sitting with Matthew at a table with a bunch of boys. Regina caught a glimpse of speckled color around his neck.

"You think he made himself another one?"

"There's only one way to find out," said Kate, hopping up with a napkin in her hand. She cruised by Teresa's table, then dropped her napkin in the trash barrel and hurried back to Margaret and Regina.

"Nothing around Teresa's neck!" she reported.

For a minute, Regina actually liked Kate. "They must have broken up!"

"Too bad," said Kate, grinning.

Regina sat back. Her campaign to make Arley miss her had worked faster than she had thought.

"Maybe he'll like you again," said Margaret.

Regina smiled. The question really was, should she like him back? After the talent show next Tuesday, she'd have tons of boys to choose from. Last night, she'd found the Black Cats.

They were in her dad's closet, just like he'd said. Regina had rooted through shoes, tennis rackets, and old high school yearbooks until she'd unearthed them under an ancient Monopoly game. The only problem now was how to light them.

She chewed her pizza, oblivious to the lunchroom din as she thought it over. Cigarettes were out. Too sickening. Matches were a no go, too. Her mom had made such a big deal about not playing with them when she was little that Regina was still terrified of them. Even if she weren't afraid, stopping to strike the matches would ruin the flow of her routine.

There had to be some way of lighting the firecrackers. And Regina the Great would think of it!

By the following Monday at the talent show rehearsal, however, the idea still hadn't come to her. She sat with

Margaret in the front row of the cafeteria, sucking on her chipped tooth as Mrs. Demetroff dimmed the lights for Teresa's performance.

With a wave to Mrs. Demetroff, Teresa Corvi's dad switched on a bank of lights. The strobe flashed, its black lights turning every white object a glowing blue.

"How do you like my teeth?" said Margaret, grinning for Regina.

"Fine, if you like blue choppers," Regina said.

On the other side of Margaret, Kate sighed. "I wish my dad would set up strobe lights for me."

Regina and Margaret exchanged a look. Kate's parents were divorced. Kate only saw her dad for a few weeks in the summer, when she flew to Colorado.

"Look at Margaret's blouse," said Regina quickly. "It's glowing."

"And the piano keys!" said Margaret.

"And Mrs. Demetroff's bra strap!" said Regina.

Kate was laughing when Teresa padded out onto the stage in jazz slippers.

Throbbing music joined the strobe lights. Teresa danced, though in Regina's opinion, not well. Where were her splits? Her walkovers? Her cartwheels? All she did was throw her arms from side to side like a hula dancer.

"You're next, Margaret," Mrs. Demetroff announced when Teresa's performance was over and the cafeteria lights went on.

Margaret walked over to the piano and, with a glance at Regina, began to play her song.

Regina swelled with pride. Though piano playing was boring, at least her best friend did it well. Margaret had made up her own song, too. She called it "Playing in the Snow with Regina," a name that certainly added to its charm. When she finished, Regina whistled and stomped her feet.

"Thank you, Margaret," said Mrs. Demetroff. "Gregory," she told a fourth-grader, "you're up next. Then Kate, you go."

"When is my turn, Mrs. Demetroff?" asked Regina.

"You're last."

Regina blinked. She couldn't believe her luck. If she couldn't be first, then last was even better. She'd be the grand finale!

There was a shuffling sound at the back of the cafeteria. Regina craned around and saw Arley and Matthew scooting over tables, punching each other on the arm.

"Boys, if you aren't in the talent show, I'm going to have to ask you to leave," Mrs. Demetroff called.

"What are they doing here?" Regina whispered to Margaret.

"Arley probably wanted to catch your act," Margaret whispered back.

Regina smiled. That was what she had thought, only she had been too modest to admit it. She'd been soundly ignoring Arley all week. He was probably going crazy.

"Broom Brain!" Matthew yelped before he and Arley ran, giggling, from the cafeteria.

Regina's hand drifted to her hairline. Her bangs had grown to the length of the tiny bristles in Lydia's eyeshadow brushes. Maybe Regina should rub them for luck like a rabbit's foot. She needed it. If she was going to blast Teresa out of the water tomorrow night, she had to figure out how to light the Black Cats, fast.

51

❀  ❀  ❀

# 10

# Silly Promises

To Regina's surprise, Mom, not Dad, was waiting in
the Rust Bucket after the rehearsal was over.

"How'd rehearsal go?" Mom asked as Regina slid
into the backseat.

"Fine." Regina didn't mention how her dance had
bored even herself without the firecrackers. "Can we
take Margaret home?"

"Sure."

Regina motioned to Margaret, who was waiting on
the sidewalk. "Come on. Get in!"

Margaret got in the car just as Kate's mother pulled
up in her red convertible. Regina rolled down her window and hung out the door. "'Bye, Kate!"

Kate waggled her fingers slowly, the corners of her
mouth drooping.

Regina shrank back into the seat, something clenching

in her stomach. Leaving out Kate didn't feel as good as she had thought it would.

Mrs. Calhoun waved at Kate's mother as they drove away. "You know her?" Regina asked.

"A little," said Mom. "She's a busy lady."

"I love watching her on TV," said Margaret.

"I love her red convertible!" Regina declared.

Mom looked at her in the rearview mirror. "Red convertibles aren't everything."

Regina made a face. How would someone who drove the Rust Bucket know?

"Boy, Arley and Teresa sure didn't last long together," said Margaret, moving her fingers over an imaginary piano keyboard as they stopped at the first traffic light.

"She wasn't his type," Regina replied. In her heart, she knew there was only one kind of girl for Arley: her kind.

"I bet I know why Arley and Matthew have been hanging around us so much lately," Regina said, wanting to share her good feeling. "Matthew likes you."

Margaret stopped moving her fingers. "No."

"He does! I know he does."

"You think so?" said Margaret hopefully.

"I know so. Why wouldn't he? You're fun."

"You're the fun one!"

"No, I'm not," said Regina modestly. Actually, Margaret was fun. Just not quite as much fun as her.

Mom cut in. "If you're wondering where your dad is, Regina, he's on an interview at Mr. Peterson's company."

Regina could feel her face heating up. She still hadn't

told Margaret about Dad losing his job. "Your song sounded good today, Margaret," she said quickly.

"Thanks. I really liked your dance, too." Margaret continued to play her imaginary piano, an absentminded look on her face.

The danger over, Regina sat back. "Wait until you see me tomorrow night. I'm adding something special."

Margaret sat up, eyes bright. She'd seen a few Regina-style specials before. "What are you going to do?"

"Yes," said Mom, frowning into the rearview mirror. "What *are* you doing, Regina?"

"It's a secret." Regina ran her tongue over her chipped tooth.

Mom chuckled. "I remember the year your kindergarten performed at the Christmas program. Ms. Wilkie should never have put you top center. Right in the middle of 'Silent Night,' you decided to cartwheel down the risers. How many kids did you take out on the way down—eight?"

"Geez, Mom. I was a baby then!"

"Well, you may be older now, but you still have a knack for getting into trouble. Promise me you won't do anything silly."

"I promise I won't do anything silly," Regina repeated, her conscience clear. Dancing around lit firecrackers wasn't silly—it was pure genius.

Regina stared out the window, dreaming of her performance the next evening. She'd throw one of the little Black Cats each time she went into a cartwheel—*bang!* Maybe she'd throw two of them when she did a backbend—*bang, bang!* At the end, she'd toss whatever firecrackers she had left, crashing down in the splits while sparks cracked around her in a Grand Finale. Bang

bang bang bang bang! She'd be better than Kate, better than Teresa Corvi, better than Fred Astaire himself!

If she could only find some way to light the firecrackers.

"Here you go, Margaret," Mom called, pulling up in front of Margaret's house.

"Thanks for the ride, Mrs. Calhoun," said Margaret, stopping to remove a piece of duct tape from her skirt. " 'Bye, Regina. Call me!"

"Okay!"

Regina rode the rest of the way home in silence. What *was* she going to do about those Black Cats?

Mr. Calhoun was drinking a glass of iced tea at the counter when Regina burst into the kitchen.

"Hi, Dad!"

"Take off your shoes, Regina."

"Oh, yeah." Regina stepped on the heels of her saddle shoes, taking them off without untying them.

"How was the interview?" asked Mom, setting her purse and keys on the counter with a clank.

"Peterson just dropped me off. His manager offered me a job."

"You take it?" Regina cried.

"Yes."

"Yay! I told you you'd get a job!"

Dad and Mom exchanged a look.

"You *did* say you got the job, didn't you?" Regina asked, uneasy. Why weren't they jumping for joy?

"I just told you I did."

Regina brightened. "Did you get a car?"

"Not this time."

Maybe that was why Dad didn't look so happy.

"Maybe you'll get one later. After our family gets one."

A corner of Dad's mouth curved up.

Mom went over and put her arms around Dad. "Don't worry, Dan. It'll be all right."

"Yeah."

Grown-ups were weird. Regina was supposed to not care about riding around in the Rust Bucket, yet they could pout about Dad not getting a new car with his job.

"So when do you start the job, Dan?" said Mom, laying a hand on his cheek.

Dad shrugged. "He said as soon as I liked. Tomorrow, I guess."

Regina cartwheeled out of the kitchen, letting her parents talk about boring job details. She spun into the family room, five cartwheels in a row, until she landed in a dizzy heap directly on top of Bones.

"Whoa, Bones!"

The dog jumped up from his spot by the air-conditioning vent. Regina stumbled to the fireplace and clutched the mantle for support. Her fingers brushed something cold. The fireplace lighter.

She whistled under her breath. "What have we found here?"

Bones cocked his head.

Gingerly, Regina picked up the wand-like instrument. She'd seen her dad use it in the winter. He'd turn on the gas in the fireplace, stick the wand by the logs, press the lever in the handle, and *poof!* a fire leapt up from the wood.

Her hands sweating, Regina gripped the lighter. Her thumb quivered over the lever. Slowly, she pressed it

56

in. A flame shot out of the top. Regina jumped, her finger slipping off the lever. The fire stopped.

Swallowing, she tried it again. The flame flicked on. She let go of the lever. It went out.

On.

Off.

On.

Off.

A smile grew on her face.

Oh, this was going to be easy.

✿   ✿   ✿

# 11

# The Secret

The next morning, Regina sat in All-school Mass, staring at the back of Teresa Corvi's neck. She had never noticed the black fuzz growing beneath Teresa's hairline. Teresa was as hairy as a monkey! No wonder Arley didn't like her anymore.

Regina glanced at her own arms. They, too, were on the hairy side, but at least she trimmed them. She took her scissors to them whenever she got bored in class—often. If only she could figure out a way of using scissors in her left hand as well as she could with her right. Her right arm was streaked with uneven patches of hair.

At the front of the church, the cantor announced, "And the recessional hymn today is on the back of your song sheets: 'Hail Regina.' "

Regina snapped to attention. *Hail Regina?*

The organ music swelled. Regina jumped to her feet.

She scanned the lyrics. She couldn't believe it. "Hail, Regina" was chockful of Hail, Reginas. She was ready when the first one came.

"Hail Regina . . . ," everyone sang.

Regina bowed deeply. "Thank you, thank you."

Margaret giggled behind her hand.

Regina grinned. She hoped Arley saw her. It wasn't often that she could entertain in church.

Those two special words floated through the air again. "Hail, Regina . . ."

Regina bobbed left. She turned to bob—Two short, thick fingers clamped on her shoulder.

"Regina, that's one detention," Mr. Amsden whispered.

Regina stopped bowing. Now that Dad was home, he had noticed her detentions. She'd better cool it. She wanted Dad to think she was as perfect as he was. Then she remembered—Dad started his new job today. He'd be too busy to notice anything . . . and he'd be making *money*. Goodbye, Rust Bucket! What a lucky day—just right for the talent show tonight.

"You better watch it around Mr. Amsden," said Margaret as the class walked across the parking lot to the school building after mass. "I think he's really getting mad at you."

"Not as mad as I'm getting at him," Regina said, running her tongue over her tooth. Secretly, she hated for Mr. Amsden to be mad. Though Dad's opinion counted most, she didn't like *anyone* to think she wasn't perfect.

Matthew darted up and poked her on the arm.

"Cooties!" cried Regina, clutching her arm. She saw her hairier arm on top. She hid it behind her back.

"Hey, Broom Brain! I've got a secret!"

"What, Stinkster?"

"No talking up there!" Mr. Amsden called from behind.

Matthew jogged ahead, his size ten-and-a-half adult's pounding the blacktop like sledgehammers. "Later, B. B.!"

"You hear Matthew?" Regina whispered to Margaret when they got in the classroom. Mr. Amsden had stopped at the drinking fountain. "He's got a secret."

Margaret smiled. "I bet it's that Arley likes you."

Regina snorted. That wasn't much of a secret. "I bet it's that Matthew likes *you*. Even though his feet are big, he is pretty cute."

Margaret twisted her palomino ponytail. "Oh, Regina."

Mr. Amsden plodded into the classroom, wiping his mouth with the back of his hand. "Okay, everyone. Get to your seats and open your Math books."

All through Math, English, and Vocabulary, Regina wiggled in her seat, wondering about Matthew's secret. The more she thought about it, the more she couldn't stand it. By lunchtime, she was ready to burst.

"Back in a minute," she told Margaret as soon as they got in the lunchline. She galloped over to Arley and Matthew, who were standing with their lunch trays, looking for a table.

"Hey," she said, tapping Matthew, "what was that secret?"

Matthew grabbed his arm. "Ooo! Broom Brain cooties."

Regina tapped him again. "Now you have double Broom Brain cooties. What's the secret?"

Arley flashed Matthew a definite *shut up* look. Mat-

60

thew smiled at Regina. "That's for me to know and
you to find out."

"No fair!"

Arley flipped back his hair. "Don't tell her,
Matthew."

Regina grinned. Though Arley had never been bashful
before, his new shyness made him cuter than ever.
"Come on, you can tell me."

"Boss says no," said Matthew. Arley started forward
with his tray.

"Sit with Margaret and me," Regina said, tagging
behind them.

Arley looked at Matthew. "You want to?"

Matthew shrugged. "Why not? As long as they don't
get their cooties on us."

"We won't," said Regina, giving Arley a knowing
look, "as long as you don't throw any pickles in my
milk."

Soon Margaret, Kate, and the boys were settled into
Regina's usual table. For old times' sake, Regina picked
a raisin out of her cookie and flung it at Arley. But
instead of winging it back, he dropped it on the floor.

What was he, sick? "What is your dumb secret, Matthew?" Regina barked.

"Don't tell her!" cried Arley, his cheeks turning
pink.

"No, tell me!" begged Regina. "You've got to tell
me! Once you say you've got a secret, you've got to
say what it is."

"Well, if I have to . . ." Matthew cleared his throat.

Arley jumped up. "I'm ordering you, Rogers!
Don't tell!"

"Oh, Matthew," said Margaret, "you don't have to

61

tell if you don't want to. We don't care, do we, Regina?''

"Not a bit." Regina swallowed. "Only—go ahead and tell me."

Kate clicked her tongue. "Oh, come on. Just tell her."

Regina pounded the table. "Tell me! Tell me! Tell me!"

Matthew shrugged. "Well, okay. Arley loves—"

Arley clamped his hand over Matthew's mouth. Regina grinned. This was better than hearing her name sung in church! "Arley loves who?"

Matthew struggled free. "Arley loves Margaret!"

# 12

# Whacking Gophers

For one strange second, nobody moved. Regina stopped breathing. The roaring lunchroom was suspended in time.

Arley pounded Matthew's arm. "I'll get you for this, Rogers!"

Matthew jumped from his seat. "You lo-ve Margaret! You lo-ve Margaret!" he yelled, Arley chasing him out of the cafeteria.

Though the lunchroom thundered and seethed around them, Regina's table was an island of silence.

"Matthew didn't mean it," Margaret said at last.

Regina stared at her lunchtray. Her chicken patties gazed back, two round orange eyes, daring her to cry.

"I don't know," said Kate. "Matthew looked like he meant it to me."

Regina glanced up long enough to see Margaret jab Kate with her elbow.

"Oh, I don't care, Margaret," Regina said. "Like him back! It doesn't matter to me."

"Oh, Regina, I could never like—"

Regina clamped her hands over her ears. "Don't say his name! I *hate* . . . you know who."

"I hate him, too!" Margaret declared.

"Not as much as I do!"

"Oh, yes I do!"

Through a mouthful of canned peaches, Kate said, "Okay, you can both hate him. Don't fight about it."

"We're not fighting!" both girls cried at once.

Kate raised a brow. "You're not?"

"No," said Regina, shoveling her oatmeal cookie in her mouth. She spat it out. Arley had touched a raisin from it.

Only Kate kept eating. After a while, she said through a mouthful of green beans, "Mom's taking me to the mall after school to get me tights for my dance tonight. Anyone want to go?" She looked at Margaret.

"No thanks," Margaret murmured. "I've got to practice my piano."

Kate shrugged. "Oh, well, thought I'd try."

Regina heard herself saying, "I'm not doing anything. I'll go."

Kate dropped her fork. "You will?"

"You will?" echoed Margaret.

"Why not?" said Regina, trying to cover her own surprise. "My act's all ready for the show."

Kate blinked. "Okay."

A weak smile flickered on Margaret's face. "You guys have fun."

Regina was still in shock after school as she waited with Kate in the parking lot. She had actually called her mother and asked to go shopping with Kate. Now she was waiting for Kate's mom to take them to the mall. Weird. But not any weirder than—

She closed her eyes. She was not going to think about Arley one more second.

Mrs. Glendenning's red convertible spun into the parking lot and purred to a stop in front of them.

"Hop in," Mrs. Glendenning said, the sun glinting on her huge black glasses. "You must be Regina. I've heard about you."

Regina's tongue flicked against her tooth. If Mrs. Glendenning heard it from Kate, it couldn't have been good.

"Come on," said Kate, climbing into the back seat. Regina scrambled in behind her.

Mrs. Glendenning twisted around and leaned towards Kate, lips puckered. Kate pulled back, scrunching against the seat. The sunglasses didn't cover Mrs. Glendenning's frown. She put the car in gear and blasted out of the parking lot, causing Regina's bird's nest to whip backward like steel wool in a wind tunnel.

"Which mall are we going to?" Mrs. Glendenning called over her shoulder.

"Northlake," muttered Kate.

"Okey-doke." Mrs. Glendenning stepped on the gas. She turned up the CD player. "You like the Eagles?" she called over her shoulder.

"Yes!" shouted Regina, not sure of who the Eagles were. It didn't matter. Being around Mrs. Glendenning made her feel like a TV celebrity herself. Lucky Kate.

They arrived at the mall. "I'll get your tights, Kate," said Mrs. Glendenning, pulling into a parking spot, "Then I've got to hurry and try on cocktail dresses."

She turned around, sucking in her breath. "I was just assigned to the opening of Planet Hollywood, Arnold Schwarzenegger's new restaurant . . . tonight."

"Tonight?" Kate cried. "My talent show's tonight!"

"I'm sorry, honey, I really am, but Kim's sick with the flu, so they gave me her assignment. I argued against taking the job, I really did, but I've got no choice. My job's on the line."

Regina looked between Kate and her mother, fearful of an explosion, but Kate sat like a rock.

"Surely someone's videotaping your show," said Mrs. Glendenning. "I'll buy a copy, then we'll watch it together, all by ourselves. Just you and me, okay, Kate?"

Kate responded by opening her door. Regina glanced at Mrs. Glendenning, unsure of what to do, but Mrs. Glendenning was already getting out of the car. "You girls meet me at the main entrance at four-thirty, okay?" she called after Kate, who was stomping toward a span of glass doors.

Regina started after Kate, her eyes huge. They were going to be in the mall *alone*? Regina's mother never let her do that. The Calhoun girls weren't allowed to go shopping by themselves until they were in the sixth grade, and then only for a half hour.

"Kate! Regina! Wait!"

Regina turned. Mrs. Glendenning held up a twenty dollar bill.

"For both of you," said Mrs. Glendenning when Regina doubled back and took the money.

"Thanks!" said Regina, torn between jumping for joy and feeling terrible. She ran after Kate, catching up inside the door of the main entrance.

"What do you want to shop for?" Regina asked, panting, when Kate finally slowed down inside by the water fountain.

Kate gave Regina a look that plainly said Dumb Question. "Candy."

Soon they were in the Candy Barrel, red wooden baskets swinging over their arms. Kate's mood seemed to improve as they made the rounds of the candy-filled barrels, dropping wrapped sweets into their baskets. Regina knew her own spirits had certainly lifted. Though she had visited the store before with her mother, she had only been allowed to pick out one piece of candy. To be able to buy ten dollars' worth at one time was heaven.

Soon they were strolling down the mall, devouring candy and venturing into stores filled with frowning clerks. A woman in Pet World asked them where their mother was. A salesman in Toy Town followed them down the aisles. The lady in Angelique's Lingerie turned them around before they reached the first rack of fancy underwear. Finally, they reached the safe harbor of the Video Arcade.

Kate slipped fifty cents into the coin slot of the "Gopher Chase" game. An electronic gopher popped out of its hole. "Play you," she said, grabbing the foam-rubber wrapped sledgehammer.

Regina shook her bag of candy as Kate whacked away. Almost empty. A sharp burp burned the back of her throat. Maybe she shouldn't have eaten so fast.

At last, the electronic gophers stilled. "Your turn," Kate said, handing over the hammer. She fed the machine two more quarters.

Regina started pounding.

"Missed those two," said Kate, leaning against the game table, her mouth full of something green and chewy. "So what do you think of Arley liking Margaret?"

"I don't care." Regina's stomach rolled. Must be the candy.

"You don't care?" Kate cried. "I would! If someone who said they were my friend stole my boyfriend, I'd care a lot."

"She didn't steal him from me."

"Hey, don't break the hammer!" said Kate, laughing. "Anyhow, I'd be mad if I were you. Margaret gets away with everything. Just because she's so sweet and goody-goody."

Regina's mouth opened and closed. Kate was right. Margaret had stolen Arley. She swallowed back a belch.

"You and me, now"—Kate smiled—"we're more alike."

"We are?" A gopher came and went, unpounded.

"Yes. We're aren't sweet and goody-goody, and we don't even try to be."

Regina lurched after a popping gopher. People didn't think she was sweet?

"Since we have so much in common," Kate said, "we ought to be best friends. Don't you think?"

Regina stood stunned. The lights went off on the machine.

"Game's over," Kate announced. "I won."

Regina held her hand over her mouth. "Can we go sit down?"

They found a bench outside the arcade in the Food Court. Kate dug in her bag for more candy, while Regina stared at the clock over the Burger Boy counter, willing its hands to move faster. She'd think about what Kate had said later, after she got home and barfed.

Kate nudged her with her elbow. "Look who just walked in."

Past a sea of black wrought iron tables, Regina recognized Margaret, trotting next to her mother.

"Miss Perfect must have finished practicing," said Kate. "Let's go see her!"

Regina stood up, her brain shouting conflicting orders. Run from Margaret! Run from Kate! Run to the restroom and hurl!

Kate grabbed her arm. "Look."

Margaret and her mother had stopped to talk to a man in a gray uniform. He was pushing a large broom, the kind Mr. Kraus used at school.

"They're talking to the *janitor*," said Kate, shaking Regina's arm. "Eeeeuuu!"

Regina squinted. The man was short and wiry. He had black hair like a bird's nest.

Margaret and her mother pointed to Regina. The man peered, then waved.

Regina jerked out of Kate's grip.

"Who is that?" said Kate.

Regina ran.

"Regina!" Kate yelled after her. "Regina, where are you going?"

Regina tore past tables and chairs, past shoppers, past babies in strollers. She ran as if racing the world until finally, blocked by a wall in the shoe department of Sears, she could run no more. She sank against a display of work boots, the burps coming up fast and scalding.

"Who was that guy?" Kate demanded, standing over her.

"You followed me?"

"He knew Margaret. He acted like he knew you."

Regina staggered to her feet. "Can we find your mom? Please? I'm sick."

Kate shrugged. "All right, but I'm not sick."

Regina ground back tears. Of course Kate wasn't sick. Her dad wasn't the janitor.

❀   ❀   ❀

# 13

# Regina vs. The World

Kate glanced at Regina, then leaned forward in the back-seat of the convertible. "Drive faster!" she shouted at her mother, who was talking on a cellular phone.

Mrs. Glendenning ended her call and lifted her hand in a salute.

Kate slumped back in her seat. Regina turned to her window. They hadn't exchanged a word since they had met Mrs. Glendenning at the mall door.

Regina knew Kate had to have figured out who the janitor was. Regina and her dad looked alike. She closed her eyes. The candy wouldn't stay in much longer.

"Home," Mrs. Glendenning said at last.

Regina scrambled out of the convertible. No one said goodbye.

In the kitchen, Regina stepped out of her shoes, then tottered toward her room. Why did she eat that candy?

The talent show was only two hours away, and her gut felt like a bubbling cauldron.

The phone rang.

"Regina!" Maureen yelled from the kitchen.

Regina sucked in her breath. "I'm busy," she yelled back.

"Just get it, Goof!"

Regina trudged to the phone. "Hello?"

"Hi, Regina," said Margaret.

"Oh. Hi."

"Want my mom to pick you up for the talent show? We're leaving at six-thirty."

"Did Kate call you yet?"

"No. Why?"

Regina's tongue hugged her tooth. Kate would never miss a chance to spread dirt. She probably called from the car the second Regina got out—they must have had a good laugh already. Why didn't Margaret just come out and say it? Regina's dad pushed a broom at Northlake!

"Regina, are you okay?"

"Why wouldn't I be?"

"I don't know. Do you want a ride?"

"No."

"You don't?" There was a strained silence. "Well, good luck tonight."

"Thanks," Regina mumbled. "Same to you." She hung up and crawled back to her bed.

Maureen strolled into the room. "Hey Goof, I thought you had a talent show tonight."

"I do," Regina groaned.

"This is your hot chance to perform in front of people

and you're laying in bed? I can't believe it. You live for this kind of stuff.''

"Have you seen Dad?"

"Dad? Uh-uh. Why?"

Regina held her stomach. "I'm sick."

Lydia stuck her head inside the door. "What's wrong with her?"

Maureen shrugged. "She's got her talent show tonight, and she says she's sick." She narrowed her eyes. "Does this have something to do with Arley?"

Regina moaned.

"Come on," said Lydia, gliding in and pulling Regina off the bed. "I don't know what your problem is, but I want to put makeup on you now before you steal it on your own."

Regina opened her mouth to object, then stopped. Makeup did sound good. Even with an upset stomach.

Later, Regina turned to the side, admiring herself in the mirror. The mascara and violet eye shadow Lydia had applied looked marvelous, as did the stiff shape Maureen had sprayed her hair into. Her new look had done wonders for making her stomachache fade. So did the bra Regina had stolen from Maureen's drawer when Maureen had left to eat dinner.

"Regina," Mom called through the locked door. "It's time to go to your talent show."

"Just a minute." Regina reached into her leotard, and sighing with regret, pulled the Kleenex out of Maureen's bra. Maybe next year. She lifted her pillow and in a swift movement, exchanged the bra for the package of firecrackers and the fireplace lighter.

Mom rattled the doorknob. "Regina? Unlock this!"

Regina tucked the Black Cats and lighter into the pocket of the shiny red soccer shorts she wore over her leotard. The firecrackers fit, but the lighter was too long.

"Regina?"

"Coming!" Desperate, Regina poked the silver wand inside the top of her leotard. She flung open the door.

"We'd better hurry," said Mom, glancing at her watch. "I'm going to drop you off, come home, grab something to eat, then come back with your dad and the girls."

Regina frowned. Did Dad have to come?

"Break a leg!" Maureen called as Regina ran past her in the kitchen.

"Make that 'break a tooth!' " Regina exclaimed. "It's luckier."

Regina sprang out of the Rust Bucket the minute it pulled up to the curb of the school. She dashed inside to the little room behind the stage where most of the other contestants were already milling around nervously in bright costumes. She bounded onto the stage and blinked into the spotlight being adjusted by Mrs. Demetroff and an eighth-grader.

She was going to win tonight, she knew it. Even if she was a Calhoun.

Kate clattered onstage in saddle shoes and a red sequined leotard. "Regina, aren't you afraid?" she squealed.

"Not really," Regina said, playing along as if they both didn't know about her father. Out of the corner of her eye she saw Margaret standing behind the curtain, watching her.

Regina scowled. Why didn't she go laughing to Arley?

Kate nudged her in the ribs. "Check out Teresa."

At the foot of the stage, Teresa's father adjusted the strobe lights while Teresa stood over him, smoothing the front of her shiny white bodysuit.

"Just think how that outfit's going to look in the strobe light," Kate whispered. "We're dead."

Regina gritted her teeth. "Not yet we're not."

Mrs. Demetroff clapped her hands. "All right! Everyone listen. It's time to line up."

"Where do we go?" asked a first-grade girl in a cowgirl outfit, sniffing back tears.

"As I told you all yesterday," Mrs. Demetroff said, putting her arm around the girl, "you are to line up by order of appearance. The first row of chairs has been reserved for you, the judges, and Mrs. Yoder and me. Everyone else will sit behind us. Okay? Let's go!"

The performers shuffled to their chairs, whispering and giggling nervously. The minute Regina took her seat, she turned around to check her audience. Instantly, she found Matthew and Arley. Matthew was staring straight at her.

"Hey, Broom Brain! Break a Broom!" He pointed to his bangs, grinning.

Regina whirled around, cheeks on fire. Wait until Matthew found out her dad pushed a broom at the mall.

The first performer, a second-grade boy, stumbled onstage to recite a poem. Three other little kids bumbled through their acts. The little girl in the cowgirl outfit sidled crab-like onto the stage and froze. Regina wanted to leap up and save her, but Mrs. Demetroff beat her to it, leading the girl away, sniffling, as the spotlight went down.

The strobe lights pulsed into action. The crowd gasped.

"Cool!" someone yelled.

"I'm glowing!" cried another.

"Look at your teeth!"

"Look at mine!"

Regina ran her tongue over her own tooth. Her dance would have to be perfect if she was going to beat Teresa. She slipped her hand into her leotard. Her secret weapon was still there.

The crowd roared when Teresa finished. Mrs. Demetroff jogged back onto stage, clapping.

"Very good. Our next contestant—" Mrs. Demetroff stopped as the crowd whistled and clapped. Finally, kids took their seats.

"Our next contestant is playing a piano melody of her own composition. She calls this piece 'Playing in the Snow with Regina.' Margaret Goodman!"

A clapping and stomping arose in the crowd. Regina turned to glare at the source. Her stomach twisted— Arley and Matthew!

Margaret bent over the piano. Butterflies bashed against Regina's gut. But why should she care how Margaret did? She wasn't even sure Margaret was still her best friend.

Margaret sailed through her piece, her fingers flitting up and down the keyboard. Regina found herself picturing playing in the blizzard with Margaret. In her mind, snowballs flew, igloos took shape, Bones barked.

The music ended.

"She wrote that *herself?*" someone said out loud.

The crowd broke out in cheers. Arley and Matthew climbed onto their chairs, leading them on. It was Arley who started the chant: "Mar-gret! Mar-gret! Mar-gret!"

Margaret hurried back to her seat, ducking her head as the crowd called her name. She slipped Regina a grin.

Regina looked away as if she hadn't seen.

Now she truly was alone against the world.

Watch out, world!

# 14

## Steppin' Out

Regina pulled out her secret weapon as Gregory Markle, a fourth-grader, made his karate moves on stage. Carefully, she peeled open the red tissue wrapper, revealing two rows of tiny firecrackers. Black Cats, glorious Black Cats. Even in the dark, she could make out the green diamond print stamped on each little cylinder. Her heart pounded. These little beauties would blast her into fame.

"Thank you, Gregory," said Mrs. Demetroff, when he had finished. "Next, Kate Glendenning will be dancing to 'I Saw A Sign.' "

Regina glanced up just long enough to see Kate pose on stage, hands under her chin, elbows out, waiting for her music. She returned to her Black Cats.

She picked up the first tiny firecracker. To her surprise, the entire bunch came with it. Her tongue flicked

78

over her tooth. She thought each little firecracker came separately. Maybe they would come apart if she gave them a good tug.

She struggled with the firecrackers until, sensing something was wrong around her, she looked up. Kate was onstage, frozen in her pose. The audience stirred in their seats.

"They can't find her music," whispered one of the contestants.

"I'm glad that didn't happen to me," Teresa Corvi said smugly.

Up in the spotlight, Kate's face congealed into pure panic. Someone belched—loudly.

Finally, Kate's music began.

Regina turned back to her problem. She held up the Black Cats to the light. They seemed to be tied together with one strong string. She gnawed furiously at the string, then stopped with a jolt. What if she bit a Black Cat and it blew up?

Tears scalded her eyes. Somehow, she had to separate the firecrackers. Fred Astaire didn't dance around one big bang. She couldn't, either.

She thought of running to her classroom and getting the scissors in her desk. The school kitchen was closer— she could get a knife.

"Mrs. Demetroff," she whispered.

"Shhh."

"Mrs. Demetroff, please!"

"Whatever it is, it can wait!"

"But—"

"Shhhhh!"

Kate finished her act. Regina was so upset she forgot to measure Kate's applause. Two more acts passed.

79

Sweat trickled down her back. Then, terribly, Mrs. Demetroff was on the stage. "And now, last, but not least, we have Regina Calhoun, dancing to the tune of 'Steppin' Out with My Baby.' "

Regina pushed off of her chair. "This ought to be good," someone cracked.

Regina's legs wobbled with fear as she climbed up the steps and into the spotlight. She tossed left arm up, hairy arm down, and waited for her music. Someone laughed. The music blasted on, startling her into motion.

" 'Steppin' out, with my baby . . .' "

Regina rolled into her first walkover, her mind in a frenzy. If she had only one big firecracker, when should she light it? At the beginning? At the end? When would Fred have lit it?

She became aware of an odd sensation. Slowly but surely, the lighter was slipping down her leotard leg. One more walkover, one more jolt, and it would drop to the floor.

She had no choice. She reached up the bottom of her shorts leg.

"What is she doing?" Mrs. Demetroff exclaimed.

Regina dug in her pocket for the Black Cats.

Mrs. Yoder leapt to her feet. "Regina Calhoun! You stop that right now!"

Regina lit the Black Cats and flung them hard—too hard. They skidded off the stage and fell at Mrs. Yoder's feet. The principal leapt backwards at the same moment Regina threw herself into the splits. The audience gasped.

Then . . . nothing. A heavy silence filled the air. The faint smell of smoke drifted by.

Mrs. Yoder crept forward and bent over the still fire-crackers. "They're duds!"

The cafeteria exploded into laughter. "REGINA!" bellowed a chorus of adult voices.

Regina bolted for the curtains. She plunged through the room offstage and outside into the night.

## 15

## "Regina Kills Matthew"

In the shadows of the school playground, Regina sank into a swing. Let some monster come and get her in the dark! What did it matter? Regina the Great had flopped.

She swung idly, wallowing in her misery, until footsteps sounded on the parking lot. Regina gripped the chains of her swing. Maybe it wasn't a monster, but worse—Mrs. Yoder coming to expel her. What if Black Cats really were illegal in Georgia? Maybe the police were coming to put her in jail.

"That swing next to you taken?"

Regina gulped. "Dad?"

Mr. Calhoun stood in front of her, his wiry figure backlit by a distant streetlight. Regina couldn't see his face in the darkness. She wasn't sure she wanted to.

"Well," he said, "do you mind if I sit down?"

Regina's teeth chattered as much from nervousness as from wearing a leotard and shorts in the cool night air. "Go ahead."

The swing creaked as Dad sat. "Well, Regina, it's been a pretty tough day for you, hasn't it?"

"Dad, I'm sorry I took your Black Cats," Regina said in a rush. "I didn't think they'd hurt anything."

"Only your reputation." Dad's swing creaked. "I imagine Mrs. Yoder will want you to stay home for a few days."

Regina sagged. She *was* getting expelled.

"You owe Mrs. Yoder an apology, Regina."

Regina nodded, swallowing back the salty rocks in her throat.

The chains of Dad's swing clinked. "Bad as that little stunt you pulled was, Regina, it's not what bothers me most."

Regina made her voice very small: "It's not?"

"I get the idea," said Dad, rocking, "that you're a little less than enthusiastic about my new job."

Regina jumped up.

"Sit down, Regina. We have to talk."

Regina sat, her tongue clinging to her tooth.

Dad sighed. "Don't worry, I'm a little less than enthusiastic about the job myself."

"Dad—it's okay!"

"It is not okay, Regina. Believe me, I know how not okay it is. I had the same kind of job when I was putting myself through college. It's not pretty work."

"Oh, Dad—"

"Just listen, would you, Regina? I didn't have any choice. We've got mortgage payments to make, food to buy—Maureen's got college in a couple years. That's not even mentioning your tuition at Queen of Angels. When Peterson offered me work, I had to take it."

"But Dad, as a janitor?" Regina clapped her hand over her mouth.

Dad laughed softly. "It's not a dirty word, Regina. It's a job, an honest job. You don't have to be ashamed."

"I know," Regina mumbled.

"You don't know. What bothers me is that you think that just because now I push a broom instead of computer buttons, I'm a different guy. Were you ashamed of me when I worked for Deskpro?"

"No." Regina sniffed. "I was proud."

"I thought so." There was a grin in Dad's voice. "We Calhouns tend to think a lot of ourselves."

Regina shuddered out a sigh. "Not this one anymore."

Dad grabbed the chain of Regina's swing. "It's the same for you. Do you think that just because you didn't pull off your firecracker act, your friends are going to think you're different? So the act didn't work—tough! You're still Regina."

Regina sucked in her breath. "I don't know if that's a good thing to be."

Dad jangled her swing. "Of course it is! You're my funny girl."

"I am?"

Instead of answering, Dad called out, "Hello-o!"

Regina sat up.

"I think it's a gentleman caller," Dad whispered.

"A what?"

"A boy."

Regina peered in the darkness. She couldn't see anything. "How do you know?"

Dad chuckled. "It takes one to know one."

Regina squinted at her father. She had never thought of him as a boy before.

"Should we hide from him?" Dad whispered, which was exactly what Regina was thinking.

A voice floated through the night. "Oh, Broom Brain!"

"Oh, no," Regina groaned. "It's Stink Breath."

Matthew stepped out of a shadow and dangled something from his hand. "Come and get your firecrackers!"

Regina sprang from her swing. "How'd you get those?"

"That's for me to know, and you to find out!" Matthew fled across the parking lot, his shoes thudding.

Regina glanced at her father, then forced herself to sit.

"The kid's obviously in love with you," Dad said.

"Stink Breath? He is not!"

Dad tapped his chest. "Remember me, the ex-boy? I know these things."

Regina jumped up. "Well, maybe I'll pound him, just for a minute."

"Go get him, Tiger," Dad called after her.

Regina sprinted through the dark, grinning. Maybe Matthew did love her. Why not? She was Regina—if not The Great, at least a survivor. Like Dad.

Margaret was in the front of the school with her mother and Kate when Regina tore by. Regina stopped so fast she nearly fell. "Margaret, you were great!" She panted a moment. "Um, you too, Kate."

"Regina, did you see who got first place?" Kate asked. She looked pointedly at Margaret's arms.

Regina's gaze dropped to the trophy locked against her friend's chest. She sucked in her breath.

"Are you mad?" asked Kate.

"Kate!" Margaret cried.

Regina's tongue flicked against her tooth. "Only a jerk would be mad."

Margaret beamed. "I knew you wouldn't be!"

Regina's cheeks burned. Good thing it was dark.

"Too bad, Regina," said Kate, shrugging. "You're in big, big trouble with Mrs. Yoder."

Regina put her arm around Margaret. She could see now why Kate was desperate to come between them. Who wouldn't want the kind of friendship Regina had with Margaret? Nobody—not Arley, not Kate, not anybody—could ever take it away.

So what was the harm in a threesome? Tentatively, she reached out her other arm to Kate. Maybe she and Kate were a *teeny* bit alike . . .

A dirt clod glanced off Regina's leg.

"Oww!" Regina exclaimed, rubbing her shin.

Matthew waved from the flowerbed by the front door of the school. "Bullseye!"

"Margaret," Regina said loudly, "write me another song, will you? Call it"—she inched towards the school door—"'Regina Kills Matthew.'"

Margaret laughed. "Okay."

Another clod pelted Regina's leg. She broke into a run. "Get ready to die, Rogers!"

"You wish, Calhoun! Get near me and I'll kiss you!"

"You better not!" Regina ran toward him faster.

As she raced, Regina reached up and touched her bangs. They were long enough now to bend back in the wind. That was the nice thing about bangs—and people, too—they grew.